MARKS &
SPENCER

BBC

Tweenies™

All Aboard the Starship Tweenie

"Telly Time!" shouted Milo. The Tweenies settled down on their beanbags. Judy was showing them a video about space.

"Where are the aliens, Judy?" asked Milo. "Hello, I am a friendly alien," he said, doing a funny alien walk and talking in a funny alien voice.

Judy laughed. "This video is all about the planets and the stars," she explained. "But if you watch carefully, you might see some aliens," she added with a twinkle in her eye.

"Oh, look! There's a rocket. And some people are getting into it," said Jake.

"They're astronauts. They travel to space in special rocket ships," explained Bella.

"And there's a big ball. Is that a planet, Judy?" asked Fizz.

"Yes, that's planet Earth. That's where we live," Judy replied.

Planet Earth was all blue and green.
"That's what it would look like if you went
high up in the sky," said Judy.

Judy pointed out the other planets.
There was a red planet, called Mars, an enormous
planet with stripes and a spot called Jupiter and
one with rings round it called Saturn.

There were other planets,
too. Each one was different.
The Tweenies couldn't believe
how amazing space was.
"And there are so many
stars, too," said Fizz.
"Can't see any aliens,
though," said Milo.

Then Judy had an idea.

"Why don't we make our own planets ?" she suggested.

"Yeah – we could make a rocket, too," said Jake.

"Then we could go on a journey into space."

So Milo, Bella and Fizz joined Judy at the messy table and they made the colourful planets.

Jake found a big box and Judy
helped him to make a rocket.

"Right. All aboard the Starship Tweenie," cried Captain Jake. Milo, Fizz and Bella joined Jake and together they zoomed up, up, up into the sky.

"Let's keep a look-out for aliens, Captain," suggested Milo. "OK," said Jake, as they sped through space.

There were some strange planets. One was spotty, one was stripy and another had flowers all over it. There was even a checked planet and a speckled one.

The Tweenies pretended they were inside a real spaceship. They had a wonderful view of space. Suddenly, they heard a strange noise.

"What's that?" said Fizz, feeling a bit scared.
"Captain, there's something on the screen," said Bella.

The Tweenies couldn't believe their eyes.
"Wow – aliens. Fab-a-rooney!" said Milo.

The aliens were jumping up and down and squeaking, squawking and babbling all at the same time.

Five aliens appeared before their eyes.
  "Thank goodness you're here," said the spotty alien.
  The flowery alien explained, "Our rocket is broken and we can't get home."

"Is there anything you can do?" asked the stripy alien.
"Pleeease? Pleeease?" pleaded the speckled alien and the checked alien.

Captain Jake didn't waste any time. "Don't worry, Captain Jake is here! Starship Tweenie to the rescue!" cried Jake. "We'll soon get you home."

"Prepare the whoosh pad," said Milo.
"Whoosh pad prepared,"
replied Bella.
"Three, two, one – GO!"
shouted Fizz.

WHOOSH!

Bella pressed the whoosh pad and whooshed
the first alien back to the spotty planet.
Then the stripy alien got whooshed back home.
Then the flowery alien, the checked alien
and, finally, the speckled alien
all got whooshed back to
their home planets.

And they were all very, very happy.

"OK. Mission complete," said Captain Jake. Fizz, Bella and Milo cheered.

"Time to go home," said Bella. "Everybody ready?"

WHOOSH!

The Starship Tweenie sped back home to planet Earth with an enormous WHOOSH!

"That was fun," laughed Fizz. "But it's good to be home!"

The Tweenies agreed that they liked their own blue and green planet best of all.

THE END